This book
belongs to -
....Jamie..Baxter...........

ISBN 0 86163 059 9

Copyright © 1975 Award Publications Limited
Spring House, Spring Place, London NW5 3BH

These Stories also appeared in
Rene Cloke's Bedtime Book of Fairy Tales and Rhymes

New Edition 1985

Printed in Hungary

Woodland Stories

Written and Illustrated by Rene Cloke

AWARD PUBLICATIONS

FAWNS IN FANCY DRESS

"The first of March!" cried Bracken the fawn, "the day of Mrs Badger's fancy dress party!"

His sister Catkin picked up the pair of fairy wings she had made the night before.

"I shall be the Spring Fairy at the party," she said. "Let's go to the woods this afternoon and gather flowers for a garland for my head."

"Good idea," answered Bracken, "I might find some more feathers for my head-dress; I'm going to be a Red Indian, we shall look a very fine pair!"

Catkin put a bottle of milk and some biscuits in a basket while Bracken painted some of the feathers on his head-dress with red and blue paint.

They trotted through the wood talking of all the fun they would have at the party that night.

"There are some primroses and a few violets," said Catkin, "I must have those."

Bracken picked a twig of hazel catkins and a bunch of periwinkles and put them in the basket with the other flowers.

After they had had their milk and biscuits and a friendly pigeon had given Bracken two loose feathers, the fawns decided to go home, but then everything began to go wrong.

Catkin saw some early kingcups growing at the edge of the river.

"Those are just what I want," she cried and galloped down to the water. The kingcups were difficult to pick and Catkin stretched too far and tumbled into the river.

Bracken helped her out and rubbed her dry.

"We'll take a short cut along this path," he said, "we mustn't be late for the party."

But the short cut was a very long one; the path turned this way and that until it grew dark and the fawns were not sure which way they were going.

"Come on," said Bracken, "through these bushes, this *must* be the way" and he bounded off.

The next moment, with a yell of terror, he disappeared. "Where are you?" screamed Catkin dashing after him and, before she could stop herself, she fell – slither, slither – down, down – bump! into a deep pit where Bracken was sitting rubbing his head.

"We shall never be able to get out of this pit," groaned Catkin.

"People in a book send a message in a bottle," said Bracken, "just throw it in the sea for someone to pick up – well, we've got a bottle!"

"But no pencil and paper," said Catkin, "and there's no sea."

Bracken thought for a moment, then he took the twig of hazel catkins from the basket and picked a piece of nearby bracken.

"I'll put these into the milk bottle," he said, "and throw it out of the pit; if anyone picks it up in the morning they'll say 'Catkin and Bracken' and look for us!"

He threw the bottle as far as he could out of the pit.

"I hope that lands on the path – it's a plastic bottle and won't break," then Bracken lay down and put his head on his knees, "I'm afraid we've missed the party" he sighed, "so we had better go to sleep."

It was morning when a cheerful voice awakened them.

"Hullo! what are you two doing down there?"

Mr Badger's face peeped over the edge of the pit.

"Just a moment, I've got a ladder in my van, I'll have you out in a jiffy."

Before long, Bracken and Catkin were scrambling up the ladder and out of the pit.

"Lucky I came this way," said Mr Badger, "I saw that bottle lying on the path and stopped to pick it up; 'Bracken and Catkin' I says, says I, those two fawns must be somewhere about and in trouble and right I was! A very clever idea of yours!"

They all clambered into Mr Badger's van.

"I drove to the wood with my ladder to gather greenery for our fancy dress party tonight," continued Mr Badger.

"Tonight?" cried Bracken and Catkin, "but yesterday was the first of March and we missed the party!"

"Ha! ha!" laughed the badger, "don't you know the old rhyme about the days of February?

'Twenty-eight are all its score,
Except in Leap Year, once in four,
February's days are one day more.'

This year is Leap Year, yesterday was the twenty-ninth of February and today's the first of March!"

"Hurray! Primroses and violets, I'll be the Spring Fairy after all!"

"Bows and arrows and tomahawks!" yelled Bracken, "and I'll be the Indian Chief!"

PAINT AND PEPPERMINT

Jeremy Squirrel walked from his cottage down to the river where his little boat lay in the rushes.

It was a bright autumn day and the leaves were floating down from the willow trees; a sharp wind sent ripples over the water and Jeremy gave a shiver.

"Winter is coming," he said, "and my boat is looking shabby; I will buy a tin of paint, light blue, I think, and paint her ready for the spring. I shall be sleeping most of the winter and I shan't want to row on the river."

He pushed his boat into the water, hopped in and took the oars.

"I'll go up the river to old Vole's shop and choose the paint," he decided.

There was great excitement in the little shop and old Vole looked very annoyed.

"Some young villain stole into my shop last night," he told Jeremy, "and took packets of chocolate, sticks of peppermint rock and bars of candy. He can't have been a very big animal, he left such small footmarks."

"I'll help you to keep a sharp look out for the thief," said Jeremy as he chose a tin of forget-me-not blue for his boat and white paint for the inside.

Spindle Hedgehog was sitting outside the shop and Jeremy, turning to speak to him as he stepped into his boat, slipped and went splash! into the water.

He was able to scramble back into his boat but he had quite a search for one of the tins of paint; at last his boat-hook caught round a handle and he was able to pull the tin from amongst the rushes.

He hung his wet shirt on the oar to dry; it made quite a good sail and Jeremy was feeling happy again by the time he reached home.

"I'll start painting at once," he decided and opened the tin of blue paint.

"What's this?" he spluttered in amazement.

Instead of blue paint, the tin held a red spotted scarf full of chocolate, sticks of peppermint rock and candy!

Jeremy dashed down to the river and pushed off in his boat.

"This will be a surprise for old Vole!"

And it was.

"After putting the stolen sweets in an empty paint tin, the thief must have heard someone coming," said the shopkeeper, "and dropped the tin in the rushes –"

"– planning to come for it later on," finished Jeremy.

"If I'm not mistaken, that scarf belongs to young Sid Shrew," said old Vole.

"Let's wait by the river tonight and catch him," suggested Jeremy, "he will find my tin of paint and think it is the one he hid."

So when it was dark the two animals hid by the waterside and, before long, a small figure crept by the river path; he began poking about amongst the rushes and gave a squeak of satisfaction as he pulled out a paint tin.

But when he opened it, he cried out in surprise.

"Not quite what you expected to find?" asked old Vole, seizing him by the collar.

Little Sid Shrew was so frightened and so surprised and puzzled and he begged so very hard to be forgiven that old Vole gave him a good lecture and let him go.

The next day Jeremy received a present and the label said –
"Dear Jeremy,
Thank you for your help.
Here is a red sail for your boat, a better one than a wet shirt!

Yours Old Vole."

PANCAKE DAY

"Bill!" cried Mrs Bobbity, "will you chop some wood for the fire, I have just finished making the carrot soup and I must go down to the market garden to get tomatoes for the salad."

Mr Bobbity looked up from his book.

"You're getting lunch ready rather early," he grumbled, "Aunt Fluffypaws won't be here yet."

"I have to mix the batter for the pancakes," answered Mrs Bobbity, tying on her bonnet, "I shall be ready only just in time."

Mr Bobbity wandered into the garden taking his book with him; it was a very exciting story and he *had* to read a few more pages before he started work.

At last the chapter was finished.

"It's getting rather late," cried Mr Bobbity and, seizing his chopper, he chopped a bundle of wood and hurried into the kitchen.

He lighted the fire and put the saucepan of soup to start cooking while he began to read the next chapter of his book.

The story became more and more exciting, the soup became hotter and hotter and at last – bubble – bubble – it boiled all over the kitchen floor!

"Horrors!" gasped Mr Bobbity.

He mopped up the floor and re-lit the fire, then he looked at the drop of soup left in the saucepan.

"Only one thing to do," he muttered, so, putting on his jacket, he hurried to the little shop next door.

He bought a large tin of carrot and parsley soup and, hiding this under his jacket, he ran home.

When Mrs Bobbity came back there was a good fire in the kitchen and the saucepan of soup waiting to be cooked.

"You stir the soup while I mix the pancake batter," she told Mr Bobbity, "and we'll soon be ready."

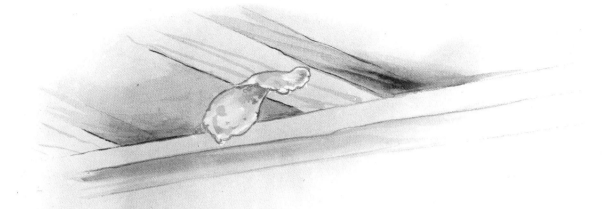

Mr Bobbity watched her tossing the pancakes and thought what fun it must be.

"Let me toss just one!" he begged.

But it wasn't as easy as it looked and he tossed the pancake so high that it stuck to the ceiling.

"How stupid you are!" scolded Mrs Bobbity, "we can't get that down without borrowing a ladder – well, perhaps it won't show stuck to the rafter. You will have to be the one to go without a second helping."

She had just finished cooking the rest of the pancakes when Aunt Fluffypaws arrived and they all sat down to lunch.

Mrs Bobbity looked hard at the soup.

"Parsley?" she murmured, "I never put parsley in my carrot soup, what can have happened to it?"

Mr Bobbity didn't notice it, he was too busy watching the pancake coming unstuck from the ceiling and then – plop – it fell lightly on Aunt Fluffypaws' hat.

Mr and Mrs Bobbity looked at each other, what *should* they do?

Mrs Bobbity tried to pick it off when she fetched the salad but Aunt Fluffypaws moved her head and she missed it. Mr Bobbity tried to pull it off when he brought the dish of pancakes to the table but it was stuck fast to a bunch of flowers on the side of the hat.

After lunch, Mr Bobbity said that he would walk home with Aunt Fluffypaws and Mrs Bobbity whispered.

"You *must* get that pancake off her hat before she sees it!"

Ten minutes later, Mr Bobbity burst into the kitchen.

"All's well!" he cried, "as we walked along the lane, dozens of birds came fluttering down and before you could say 'Winkypop' they'd pecked all the pancake off Aunt Fluffypaws' hat! She was so interested in the exciting story I was telling her that she didn't notice what was happening."

Mrs Bobbity gave a sigh of relief.

"But I'm still puzzled about that soup," she said, "it certainly didn't taste like my usual carrot soup and I know I didn't put in any parsley."

Mr Bobbity crept out into the garden; he cut up the empty soup tin into little pieces and threaded them on a string to keep the birds off his lettuces.

Then *he* gave a sigh of relief.

"No need for anyone to know about that," he said.

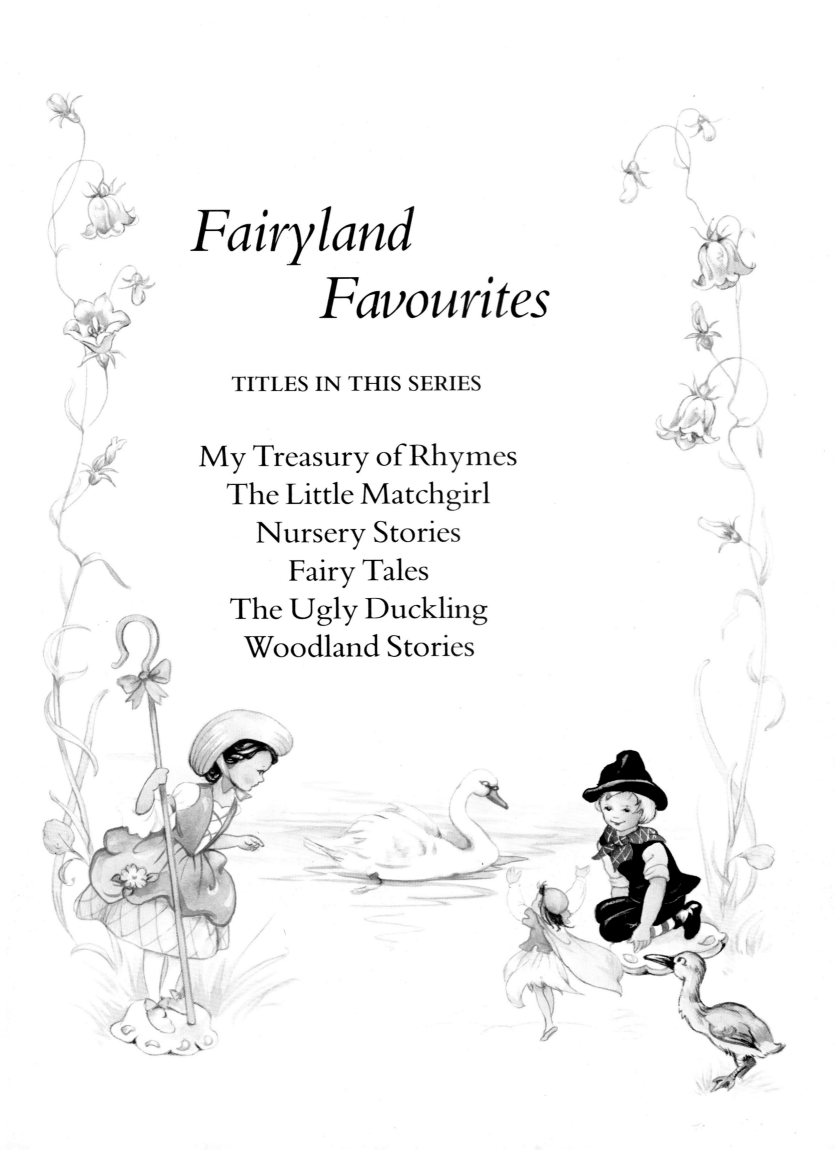

Fairyland Favourites

TITLES IN THIS SERIES